Anne of Green Gables

Retold by
Sally Morgan

Illustrated by
Mel Howells

ARCTURUS

To Lily, Daisy, and the many kindred
spirits in my life—SM.

For Rachel—MH.

This edition published in 2018 by Arcturus Publishing Limited
26/27 Bickels Yard, 151–153 Bermondsey Street,
London SE1 3HA

Writer: Sally Morgan
Illustrator: Mel Howells
Designer: Jeni Child
Editor: Susannah Bailey
Art Director: Jessica Crass

ISBN: 978-1-78828-682-4
CH006276NT
Supplier 24, Date 0318, Print run 6727

Printed in Malaysia

Contents

CHAPTER 1
An Arrival at Green Gables

One sunny afternoon in June, Mrs. Rachel Lynde was sewing at her kitchen window when she noticed something she thought surprising—her friend, Mr. Matthew Cuthbert, wearing his best suit and driving his buggy over the hill out of Avonlea.

Well, if that isn't Matthew Cuthbert of Green Gables, Mrs. Rachel thought. *What could he be doing leaving Avonlea when he should be sowing his turnip seed like the other farmers?*

It was for events such as these that Mrs. Rachel liked to work at her window, which was in such a position that little went on in Avonlea without her knowing about it. From here, she was able to keep her all-seeing eye on everything going on in and around the town.

I'll walk over to Green Gables and ask Marilla where he's gone and why, she decided. *I won't find a minute's peace until I know what has taken Matthew Cuthbert out of Avonlea today.*

After tea, Rachel stepped into the lane. Green Gables was not far, even though it was at the very edge of town.

"Good evening, Rachel," said Marilla, "Do sit down. How are all you folks?"

"We're all well," said Rachel. "I was afraid you weren't, when I saw your brother Matthew out in the buggy. I thought he'd gone for the doctor."

Marilla had expected this visit. Matthew seldom went visiting, and she knew that the sight of him, out in his best suit, would be too much for her friend's curiosity.

"I'm fine," she said. "Matthew went to the station at Bright River. We're getting a boy from an orphanage to help us at Green Gables."

"An orphan!" exclaimed Mrs. Rachel. "What can you be thinking? Didn't you

read about the little orphan girl who poisoned her adoptive family?"

"I did not," replied Marilla. "But we're not getting a girl. And we need help—the farm is a lot of work for an old man."

Mrs. Rachel wanted to stay until Matthew returned, but after realizing he wouldn't be back for hours, she went to tell a friend the important news that an orphan was coming to Green Gables.

When Matthew Cuthbert arrived at
Bright River, he walked up to the station.

"I'm here to meet the 5:30 train," said
Matthew to the stationmaster.

"You've missed it," the stationmaster
replied. "But there's a passenger for
you. She's waiting on the platform."

"She?" Matthew
scratched his head.
"I'm expecting a boy."

"You'd better
ask her," smiled the
stationmaster. "She'll
explain."

Matthew walked onto the platform
and approached the thin girl with red
hair who was waiting for him.

"You must be Mr. Cuthbert," she said,
putting out her hand. "My name is Anne

Shirley. I was hoping you would come soon but decided if you didn't, I would spend the night in one of those beautiful cherry trees. Don't you think it would be wonderful to spend the night in a cherry tree, Mr. Cuthbert?"

"Well, I don't know," answered Matthew, deciding then and there that he could not tell her there had been a mistake. Instead he led Anne to the buggy.

"I can't wait to see Green Gables," said Anne. "I think it's wonderful that I'm going to live with you. The orphanage was worse than any place you can imagine. Mrs. Spencer said it was wicked of me to talk that way. It's so easy to be wicked without even knowing it. I do try to be good. Would you rather be divinely beautiful, dazzlingly clever, or angelically good? I could never be divinely beautiful. Mr. Cuthbert, how would you describe my hair?" Anne held up a thick braid.

"Red?" answered Matthew.

"Exactly," sighed Anne. "I can imagine almost anything away except my red hair. Am I talking too much?"

"Oh, I don't mind," answered Matthew, who was enjoying the girl's chatter.

Anne continued talking until they

arrived at Green Gables, a pretty white house surrounded by trees.

"Who is this? Marilla asked, startled by the girl in her kitchen. "Where is the boy?"

Matthew explained that there was only Anne.

"Well, there has been a mistake," said Marilla. "She can sleep here tonight, but tomorrow I will take her to Mrs. Spencer."

"You don't want me!" cried Anne. "You don't want me because I'm a girl?"

"What is your name, child?" asked Marilla.

"Please could you call me Cordelia?" answered Anne.

"Call you Cordelia? Is that your name?"

Anne explained that as she wasn't going to live at Green Gables, she would like to be called Cordelia while she was there.

"I've got no time for nonsense," said Marilla, sternly. "What is your name?"

"Anne," said Anne, disappointed. "But please could you be sure to spell it with an 'e' when you say it?"

Then, they sat down to dinner, after which Marilla took Anne to a small, neat bedroom. Anne immediately threw herself face first onto the bed and sobbed loudly.

"There, there, child," Marilla said awkwardly. "We will sort this all out first thing tomorrow. Get yourself dressed for bed, and I'll be back in a minute to take out the candle."

The next morning, after breakfast, Marilla and Anne climbed into the buggy to drive back out to Mrs. Spencer.

CHAPTER 2

A Surprise for Anne

"I didn't expect to see you today," said Mrs. Spencer, as Marilla helped Anne down from the buggy. "How are you, Anne?"

"As well as can be expected," Anne answered, before Marilla went on to explain the mistake that had been made.

"Do you think the orphanage will take her back?" Marilla asked.

"Of course," Mrs. Spencer answered. "But I don't think we will have to. Mrs. Blewett was here yesterday saying she wished I had brought her a girl to help with her many children. What good luck—here she is now!" said Mrs. Spencer, as a woman pulled up. "Mrs. Blewett, this is Anne."

"She's skinny," said Mrs. Blewett, "but the

wiry ones can be strong. I'll take her. I need help with my youngest child—she cries a lot."

"Well, I don't know," said Marilla, seeing Anne looking pale. "We hadn't absolutely decided not to keep her. Let me check with Matthew, and I will let you know."

Marilla didn't know Mrs. Blewett well, but she'd heard that she treated workers unkindly. Returning Anne to the orphanage was one thing—handing her to someone like Mrs. Blewett was another!

"Did you mean it?" asked Anne on the drive back. "Might you let me stay with you and Matthew?"

"I said I hadn't made up my mind," said Marilla. "Now, stop talking, and give me some peace."

Later, while helping Matthew with the cows in the barn, Marilla told Matthew what had happened with Mrs. Spencer.

"I wouldn't give a dog to that Blewett woman," said Matthew.

Marilla agreed, but it was either that or let the girl remain at Green Gables.

"I guess she will have to stay with us," sighed Marilla. "We'll tell her tomorrow," she added.

Matthew grinned.

The next day, Anne held her tongue until she could wait no more.

"Please, Miss Cuthbert," Anne asked while washing dishes. "Please will you tell me whether or not you are going to keep me? I really must know!"

"We have decided that we will," Marilla replied, "if you promise to be a good girl and show yourself grateful."

"Oh, Miss Cuthbert!" cried Anne. "I promise I'll do my best to be good."

Anne kept her word and was very well behaved for two weeks. Then, Mrs. Rachel came to visit.

"Why, Marilla," Mrs. Rachel said, looking Anne over. "Her hair is as red as carrots!"

Anne flushed red with anger. "I hate you! I hate you, I hate you!" Anne shouted loudly, stamping her foot.

"Go to your room, Anne," Marilla ordered, before turning to Mrs. Rachel. "You were too hard on her, Rachel."

"Well, I see I will have to be very careful about what I say in this house!" said Mrs. Rachel, sounding hurt. "Good day, Marilla."

When Anne didn't come down for dinner, Matthew went up to speak to her.

18

"Mrs. Rachel shouldn't have spoken to you that way," Matthew said, "but you were rude, and you should apologize."

"If you say I must," Anne said, "I will. But I can't promise that I will mean it."

The next morning, Anne and Marilla went to see Mrs. Rachel, and Anne made a very thorough, if slightly overdone, apology. Mrs. Rachel took pity on her and told Anne that she knew a girl who had hair redder than hers,  which had turned a beautiful auburn. From that moment on, they became friends.

CHAPTER 3

Friends and Enemies

A week or so later over breakfast, Marilla told Anne some good news.

"I was talking to Mrs. Barrie after church," Marilla said, "and she thought you might want to meet her daughter, Diana. I could take you over to meet her this afternoon, if you'd like."

"I've always wanted a best friend!" said Anne, almost knocking over her milk. "I had an imaginary friend named Katie at the orphanage but never a real one!"

Marilla had tea with Mrs. Barrie that afternoon, leaving Anne and Diana to get to know each other in the rose garden.

Diana liked Anne very much, and the two girls found they had a lot to talk about.

"Let us swear to be best friends forever," said Anne, before she was about to leave.

"It's wicked to swear," said Diana, looking worried. "Though, I would like to be friends."

"This is a good kind of swearing," said Anne. "It's a promise—it's not wicked at all."

So, the girls held hands over the path in Diana's rose garden and promised to be best friends until the end of time.

Anne and Diana played together all around Avonlea every day that summer. When September came, the girls walked to the school house arm in arm, and Diana introduced Anne to all of her friends.

"That's Gilbert Blythe," Diana said, pointing to a dark-haired boy who was grinning from the other side of the yard. "Don't you think he's handsome?"

Anne didn't get a chance to answer as their teacher, Mr. Phillips, rang the bell.

Anne did her best to concentrate on the lesson, but Gilbert Blythe was determined to get her attention.

"Hey, Anne," he whispered, "Anne!"

When Anne pretended she couldn't hear, Gilbert reached out and pulled one of Anne's braids.

"Carrots!" he whispered, grinning.

"How dare you call me 'carrots'!" Anne yelled as whole class stared.

Gilbert had begun to apologize, when Anne picked up the slate and smashed it hard over his head.

"Anne Shirley!" Mr. Phillips shouted. "Stand in front of the board for the rest of the day." He took a piece of chalk and, spelling her name in the way Anne hated, wrote, "Ann Shirley has a very bad temper" in large letters above her head.

When Mr. Phillips let the class out for the day, Anne raced out of the door with Diana trailing behind.

"I'm sorry, Anne!" Gilbert called after them. "I didn't mean to hurt your feelings."

Anne ignored him and marched home with her head held high.

"Oh, Anne. Gilbert teases all the girls. He always calls me 'Crow Head,'" Diana explained, holding out a lock of her own dark hair. "But I've never heard him apologize before."

"Gilbert has hurt my feelings immeasurably, and I will never forgive him," said Anne.

At home, Anne ran into the kitchen and told Marilla that she would not be returning to school and that nothing Marilla said would change her mind. Mrs. Rachel visited before dinner, having heard what had happened to Anne.

"Give her time," Mrs. Rachel said. "She's a bright girl and will go back to school when she's ready. No sense forcing her." Mrs. Rachel had had many children, and so Marilla took her friend's advice.

The next morning, Diana made the walk to school alone, leaving Anne at home with Marilla.

Anne did not return to class. She busied herself with helping around the farm and played with Diana in the evenings. Diana told her all the news from school, without making any mention of Gilbert Blythe.

One Saturday morning in the winter, Marilla told Anne that she would be out for the evening and wondered if she would like to invite Diana over for tea. "You can serve some of my raspberry cordial, if you would like," Marilla added.

"Yes, please!" Anne cried.

Anne baked a cake. Then, even though Marilla said they would make a mess, she brought in flowers from the garden. She wanted to be the perfect hostess.

After Diana arrived, the pair chatted for a while before Anne remembered the cordial. She poured Diana a large glass.

"It's delicious," said Diana. "Much better than Mrs. Lynde's."

Anne smiled and quickly poured her friend another glass—and then another. Diana drank two more large glasses.

"Why, Diana," Anne said, noticing that her friend looked unwell, "are you okay?"

"No," Diana slurred. "Must. Go. Home."

Anne watched in dismay as her friend stumbled toward the door and left!

"Your Anne got my Diana drunk, Marilla," Mrs. Barrie said, when she called by the next morning. "I have forbidden Diana from playing with her. I was worried about my Diana being friends with an orphan, and I was right!"

"Drunk?" Marilla said. "That's impossible. All they had was tea and raspberry cordial."

Marilla fetched the bottle to show Mrs. Barrie, but when she looked more closely at it, she saw that Anne had mistakenly picked up an old bottle of redcurrant wine!

Marilla pleaded with Mrs. Barrie, pointing out that it had been her mistake and not Anne's, but Mrs. Barrie had made up her mind. Anne was a bad influence on her Diana and they were not to play together any longer.

When Marilla told Anne what Mrs. Barrie had said, Anne ran straight to her room and cried until she thought her heart would break.

The next morning was Monday, and Marilla was surprised to see Anne at the breakfast table with her textbooks sitting next to her.

"I have decided that I will go back to school," Anne said to an astonished Marilla.

CHAPTER 4
A Test of Friendship

Winter brought a thick layer of snow to Avonlea, and Anne and Diana had to make the cold trudge to school alone.

At school, Anne and Diana no longer sat together and shared secrets as they had before, and though Anne got along well with the other girls in Mr. Phillips's class, she wanted her old friend back.

One person who did want to make friends was Gilbert Blythe. Gilbert tried to make it up to Anne by giving her a sugar heart, but Anne was stubborn. She placed the candy under her shoe and ground it into powder.

Without Diana, Anne worked hard at her studies. She was smart and caught up with the rest of the class quickly. She often found herself in a tie with Gilbert for the best marks. Sometimes, Gilbert would come first in spelling, then Anne. Whenever Gilbert did come first, Anne would study even harder that night to make sure she beat him the next day.

Anne missed her best friend dearly, but she tried hard to keep herself busy and hoped that one day soon they would be reunited.

Anne had to wait until January before Diana made an unexpected visit. All was calm at Green Gables, as a blanket of snow fell. Marilla had gone out of Avonlea with Mrs. Rachel and many other townsfolk to hear the prime minister speak. Anne and Matthew were enjoying an evening by the fire, when an upset Diana appeared.

"Do come quick, Anne!" Diana begged. "Minnie May is sick—she's got croup and can hardly breathe. Father and Mother are out of town. Anne, I am so frightened she will die."

Without a word, Matthew put on his coat and hat and slipped out the door to get the doctor.

Anne ran to gather medicine from the pantry. "Please don't cry, Diana. I know exactly what to do for croup. You'll see. Minnie May will be better in no time."

Anne wasn't so sure when she saw how sick Diana's little sister was.

Anne cradled Minnie May on the sofa and gave her some medicine as she had done for the children at the orphanage before she came to Green Gables. She prayed the doctor would come soon.

The two friends nursed a very sick Minnie May through the night, using up all of the medicine Anne had brought. Anne wasn't sure that Minnie May would make it, until the little girl gave a mighty cough and was able to breathe easily again. By the time Matthew arrived with the doctor in the morning, Minnie May was sleeping soundly in Anne's arms.

The doctor examined Minnie May and was sure the two young nursemaids had saved her life.

Anne went to bed and slept well into the afternoon. When she did come down, Marilla had returned and told her that Mrs. Barrie had stopped by to ask Anne if she would be so kind as to call on her when she woke up.

"Please can I go right away?" Anne

asked, hoping Mrs. Barrie had forgiven her.

Anne didn't wait for an answer but ran out into the snow without her coat.

At Diana's house, Anne was invited into the living room. Mrs. Barrie cried and told Anne how grateful she was to her. She also added how sorry she was that she ever believed Anne had made Diana drunk on purpose.

So, Anne and Diana were friends once more, happy to be able to walk through the wintry woods to school. As they walked, they made up stories and planned adventures to go on when the weather got warmer.

When summer arrived and school was coming to an end, Mr. Philips told their class he would not be returning to teach them in September and that they would be getting a new teacher instead.

Anne and Diana were so beside themselves with sadness that they cried all the way home on his last day.

"I can't say that I particularly loved Mr. Philips," Anne said, before blowing her nose into her handkerchief and remembering her horrible first day, "but I do so hate to say goodbye to anybody."

"Me, too!" Diana sobbed. "I am sure we won't like the new teacher as much as Mr. Phillips. But at least we have a nice, long summer to look forward to."

And then, the two girls quickly forgot their sadness over Mr. Philips as the talk turned to picnics, boat rides on the pond, and apple picking.

CHAPTER 5

New Lessons

When the new teacher, Miss Stacy, did arrive in Avonlea, people dutifully took turns inviting her over for tea before the next school year began.

"Please, may I bake a cake, Marilla?" Anne begged, excited to meet her new teacher. "I'm much better at baking now."

Anne followed the recipe faithfully and almost wore a hole in the rug as she paced up and down in the kitchen, waiting to see how it would turn out.

"Why, Anne," said Miss Stacy, smiling as Marilla poured the tea, "if you made the cake, be sure to cut me a nice, big piece."

Marilla, however, looked horrified when she took a bite of her slice. The cake didn't

taste good at all. Anne had mistaken a
bottle of antiseptic ointment for vanilla!

"How could you be so careless, Anne?"
Marilla tutted, gathering up the plates.
"It's time you got serious and stopped
daydreaming."

"I am so sorry, Miss
Stacy!" Anne cried.
"I wanted to
make a good
impression,
and for you
to like me!"

"You did make a good impression,"
Miss Stacy laughed. "In fact, I am here
because Mr. Philips recommended that
I ask Mr. and Miss Cuthbert if you could
join a special class that would help you
study to become a teacher."

Miss Stacy explained this special class to Marilla and Matthew. Anne and the other students selected to be in the class would stay behind after school each day and study for the entrance exam to Queen's Academy. If Anne did well and passed, she would be able to attend the academy and study to be a teacher—just like Mr. Phillips and Miss Stacy!

Matthew and Marilla agreed Anne should join the class. They thought it was important for Anne, who had no family of her own, to be able to make her own way in the world. Anne was thrilled. She thought she would like being a teacher very much and promised to work hard.

Anne was less excited to discover that Diana would not be in the class. Mrs. Barrie did not want Diana to become a teacher but preferred that she learn how to keep a nice home instead.

So, the two girls still walked to school together, but when the day was over, Diana left Anne with the rest of the Queen's class—a class that included Gilbert Blythe ...

Anne did well with Miss Stacy as her teacher and found that she enjoyed her studies in a way she never had with Mr. Phillips. Miss Stacy encouraged the class to ask questions, exercise outdoors, and recite poetry—all things that Anne adored.

"I love Miss Stacy with my whole heart, Marilla," Anne said, when she came home from school one day. "She is so sweet. I feel instinctively that when she says my name, she is spelling it with an 'e.'"

Things got even more exciting for the class in November, when Miss Stacy announced that they were to put on a concert to raise money for a new flag for the school. Diana was to sing a solo, and Anne was to recite two poems. Anne couldn't wait for the performance.

"Can you imagine, Marilla," Anne said over dinner, "your Anne standing up in front of all those people? I only wish I had a dress with puffed sleeves like the other girls. Don't you hope I will do well?"

"I just hope that you behave yourself," replied Marilla, who didn't believe children should be running around putting on concerts when they should be studying. "And as for puffed sleeves, your Sunday dress will do well enough."

After dinner, Matthew thought about what Anne had said. He had seen her with her friends, and Anne looked different. He hadn't been sure what it was, but now he knew—it was the puffed sleeves! Marilla had made all Anne's clothes in the same plain style as her own, whereas her friends wore frills, puffs, and bows.

Matthew wanted to do something, and so, the next evening, he drove to town.

"What can I get for you, Mr. Cuthbert?" asked the assistant in the store.

Matthew froze. He was not used to talking to women who weren't his sister, Anne, or Mrs. Rachel.

"Um," he stumbled, "do you have any garden rakes?"

The assistant said she would have to check, since they didn't sell many in

November. Nor did they have hayseed,
which Matthew asked for next.

Matthew left with a rake and twenty
pounds of brown sugar—but no dress.

On the way home, he stopped in on
Mrs. Rachel.

"Please let me choose a dress for Anne,"
said Mrs. Rachel, when Matthew told her
what he wanted. "It will be lovely to see
her wearing something decent for once!"

Mrs. Rachel bought a pretty brown dress for Anne and took it to Green Gables the night before the concert. Marilla, who had known Matthew was up to something, did not approve.

"She'll be as vain as a peacock now, Matthew," Marilla said, thinking of the simple dresses she had just made for Anne. "You could make a whole dress from just one of those sleeves!"

Anne, however, did approve. So much so, that for once, she was speechless as her eyes filled with tears.

"Don't you like it?" Matthew asked.

"Like it?" Anne said in wonder. "It's perfect!"

The concert was a triumph. All of Anne's friends told her her speech had been a huge success, but Anne wasn't so sure, and had to be convinced.

"I thought for a moment that I wouldn't be able to begin," Anne explained. "Then, I thought of my lovely puffed sleeves and took courage. I knew that I must live up to those sleeves."

Gilbert Blythe had also read his piece well, and though Anne claimed she hadn't noticed, he had certainly taken notice of her and clapped wildly when she took her bow.

Avonlea's cold winter melted into spring. This was when the real work of the Queen's class began, and when June finally came, Anne took the entrance exam.

Anne thought she would rather fail than not come high on the list, and by high, she meant higher than Gilbert.

However, she was determined not to worry about the results and to enjoy her summer. So, this was how one afternoon, Anne and her friends ended up playing "The Lily Maid" on the Barries' pond.

Anne was to be the dead Lily Maid and lie under a blanket strewn with flowers

at the bottom of Mr. Barrie's boat. Her friends, the mourners, were to push the boat into the water, so that it drifted to the little beach, where Anne could get out.

All went well until, not long after setting sail, Anne felt water beneath her. She was sinking! As she floated toward the bridge, Anne climbed out and clung to a post, wondering what to do next.

Anne didn't have to wonder long, because also enjoying the pond that day was Gilbert Blythe, who rowed over and helped her into his boat.

"I do hope this means we can be friends now, Anne," Gilbert said, pulling up onto the beach.

"It does not," Anne said. "Now, if you will excuse me, I must go find Diana and tell her that I am alive."

When Anne's boat hadn't arrived at the little beach, Diana had run to Green Gables in search of Matthew.

"I thought you had drowned!" Diana cried, embracing her friend.

"I'm quite alright, Diana," Anne said, still dripping wet. "The boat sank, but Gilbert was on the pond and rowed me back."

"How romantic of him!" Diana sighed. "Surely you must forgive him now?"

"I will not," Anne said. "And I don't want any talk of romance. Romantic ideas are what had me thinking I could be the Lily Maid in the first place!"

Just then, Mrs. Rachel came walking up the path with Matthew and Marilla.

"You might want to take a look at this, Anne," Mrs. Rachel said, smiling and handing Anne the results paper.

Anne took it, but was too scared to read what was written.

"Please will you look?" Anne begged.

Diana studied the list.

"You passed, Anne!" she cried, hugging her friend. "You can go to Queen's Academy! And you tied for first out of a list of two hundred! With Gilbert!"

"You've done pretty well, Anne," Marilla said.

"She's done very well, Marilla!" Mrs. Rachel corrected. "Very well indeed, Anne!"

CHAPTER 6

A Bend in the Road

The summer passed by too fast for Anne.
The final weeks were spent getting
everything ready to go to the Academy.
There was sewing to be done and
arrangements to be made. Anne needed
new dresses, and Marilla even bought her
a beautiful green one, complete with as
many frills and puffs as Anne could ever
have wished for.

"I thought you might want something
fancy to wear if you were asked out in the
evening," she said, as she gave it to Anne.

Anne tried it on and recited a poem
for her and Matthew. When she finished,
Marilla was crying.

Once everything was packed, Anne

said her goodbyes around Avonlea before stopping at Diana's for the hardest goodbye of all ...

When she got back to Green Gables, Matthew was resting at the gate. He'd become a lot older over the years, and now every day seemed to make him more tired.

"I do wish that I had been that boy you had sent for," Anne said, walking him into the house, "so that I could have helped you more."

"I'd rather have you than a dozen boys," Matthew said, smiling. "You're our girl, Anne."

The next morning, Matthew drove Anne to the station where she was to meet the other Avonlea students, so that they could travel together to Queen's.

The first days were a whirl of excitement, as they were all arranged into classes. Anne and Gilbert found that they were to be in the same class, since they were both to study the two-year course in a single year. Anne wasn't sure what she would have done without him as her rival.

As the term wore on, Anne made new friends, though none were as dear to her as Diana. And she never stopped missing her beloved Green Gables.

To distract from her loneliness, Anne threw herself into her studies. She was determined to win one of the prizes awarded to the very best students. One of the prizes was a scholarship to the university.

Anne took her exams at the end of the year and once again found herself waiting impatiently to find out how she had done.

But when the big day came, she was again too frightened to read the results!

"I can't look," Anne said to her classmate, Jane, as they walked to where the results were posted. "You must read the announcement and then come and tell me. If I have failed, just say so."

Jane promised, but she needn't have, because as they approached the steps, they saw a crowd of boys carrying none other than Gilbert Blythe on their shoulders.

"Hurrah for Gilbert Blythe!" a voice cried. "Winner of the gold medal!"

Anne's heart sank for a moment. She thought that Gilbert had won a prize and she had not.

But then she heard … "Three cheers for Anne Shirley! Winner of the scholarship!"

Anne couldn't believe her ears. She had won, and more than that, she would be going to study at a real university!

With Queen's Academy over, Anne was delighted to return home and enjoy the summer at Green Gables. She had not been back since April, and she longed to see the blossom in the apple orchard and all the delights of Avonlea.

"Oh, Diana, it's so good to be here," she said, as they picked armfuls of flowers along the path. "I will be so sad to leave when college starts."

"Did you hear that Gilbert's not going?" Diana said, "His father can't afford to send him this year, so he is going to teach at Avonlea."

"I didn't," Anne said, dismayed. She had hoped to resume their old rivalry.

When Anne got back to Green Gables, she took her flowers into the kitchen and was looking for something to put them in when she heard a shout.

"Matthew ... Matthew!"
Marilla cried. "Matthew,
are you sick?"

Anne dropped the
flowers and ran to
Marilla. She found
her with Matthew,
who had fallen and
looked very pale.

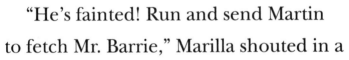

"He's fainted! Run and send Martin
to fetch Mr. Barrie," Marilla shouted in a

panic, trying to bring
Matthew around.

Anne sent Martin,
the farmhand, to fetch
Mr. Barrie and met
Mrs. Rachel on her
way back to Marilla.

On the porch, Mrs. Rachel gently pushed Marilla aside and laid her head over his heart to check for his pulse.

"I don't think ... I don't think we can do anything for him," Mrs. Rachel said gravely.

"Mrs. Lynde," Anne started. "You don't mean ... Matthew is ..."

"I'm afraid so," Mrs. Rachel replied, tears in her eyes. "Matthew is dead."

That night in her bed, Anne wept, thinking of her dear Matthew who had been so proud of his girl. Marilla heard and crept in to comfort her.

"How will we go on without him?" Anne sobbed.

"We've got each other," Marilla said. "You may think I have been strict with you, Anne, but you mustn't think I loved you any less than Matthew. You've been my joy since you came to Green Gables."

Two days later at the funeral, they carried Matthew away from Green Gables, away from the fields he had tilled and the trees he had planted.

Avonlea returned to normal, although Anne found it strange that things could continue as before without Matthew.

But not everything had settled back to how it was. Marilla's eyesight was failing, and as an old woman, she would not be able to manage Green Gables. Marilla felt she had no choice but to sell it.

"You absolutely mustn't sell Green Gables," Anne said decisively.

"I wish I didn't have to," Marilla said. "But I can't stay here alone."

"You won't be alone," Anne told Marilla and Mrs. Rachel, who had come to call. "I'm not going to go to the university. I'm going to stay and teach at the school in Carmody. I can travel home each day and help you."

"You will do so no such thing," Mrs. Rachel corrected. "You're going to stay and teach in Avonlea. Gilbert is going to take the Carmody school."

Mrs. Rachel explained that when Gilbert had heard about the situation, he insisted the closer Avonlea school be given to Anne.

"How will I ever thank him?" Anne wondered, amazed.

"You better think of something, Anne." Marilla smiled. "He's coming down the road right now."

Anne rushed after Gilbert.

"Gilbert," Anne gasped when she caught up with him. "I want to thank you for giving up the school for me."

Anne offered him her hand, and Gilbert took it, saying he hoped they could be friends now. Anne nodded, happy to have forgiven him.

Gilbert walked Anne back to Green Gables, where they stood at the gate in the warm evening, catching up on their lost years of friendship and promising to share many more in Avonlea.